WHERE THE FOREST MEETS THE SEA

story and pictures by Jeannie Baker

Greenwillow Books, New York

Artwork photographed
by Philip Mandalidis
and David Blackwell

Printed in Singapore by Tien Wah Press
First American Edition 21 20 19 18

Library of Congress Cataloging-in-Publication Data
Baker, Jeannie. Where the forest meets the sea.
Summary: On a camping trip in an Australian rain forest
with his father, a young boy thinks about the history of
the plant and animal life around him and wonders about
their future. [1. Rain forests—Fiction. 2. Australia—
Fiction] I. Title. PZ7.B1742Wh 1987 [E] 87-7551
ISBN 0-688-06363-2 ISBN 0-688-06364-0 (lib. bdg.)

To David,

with all my love

My father knows a place
we can only reach by boat.

Not many people go there,
and you have to know the way through the reef.

When we arrive, cockatoos
rise from the forest
in a squawking cloud.

My father says there has been a forest here
for over a hundred million years.

My father says there used to be crocodiles here,
and kangaroos that lived in trees.
Maybe there still are.

I follow a creek into the rain forest.

I pretend it is
a hundred million years ago.

On the bank of the creek, the vines and creepers try to hold me back.
I push through. Now the forest is easy to walk in.

I sit very still.
...and watch.
...and listen.

I wonder how long it takes the trees
to grow to the top of the forest!

I find an
ancient tree.
It is hollow.
Perhaps
aboriginal
forest children
played here,
too.

I climb inside the tree.
It's dark,
but the twisted roots make windows.
This is a good place to hide.

It is time to go and find my father.
I think I hear the sea.
I walk towards the sound.

My father has made a fire
and is cooking the fish he caught.

I like fish cooked this way.
But then I feel sad
because the day has gone so quickly.
My father says we'll come here again someday.

But will the forest still be here when we come back?

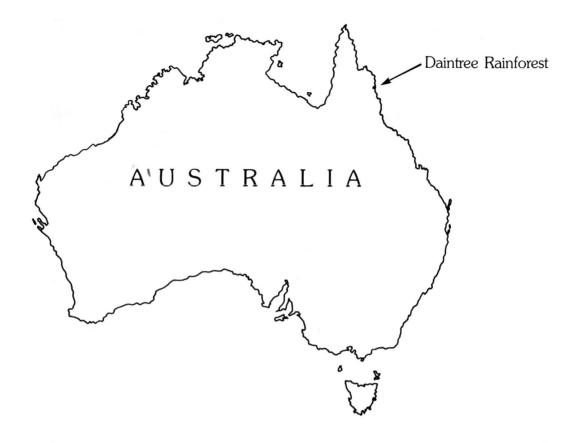

Daintree Rainforest

AUSTRALIA

The place, the people, and the predicament are real. This forest is part of the wilderness between the Daintree River and Bloomfield in North Queensland, Australia. There remain at the making of this book only 296,000 acres of *wet* tropical rain forest wilderness that meet the ocean waters of the Great Barrier Reef. Small as it is, this is the largest pristine area of rain forest left in Australia.

The artist made two extensive field trips to the Daintree Wilderness to research and collect materials.

These relief collages are constructed from a multitude of materials, including modeling clay, papers, textured materials, preserved natural materials, and paints.

The collages are mostly the same size as the reproductions.